Opera Cat

Clarion Books
a Houghton Mifflin Company imprint
215 Park Avenue South, New York, NY 10003
Text copyright © 2002 by Thérèse W. Gullickson
Illustrations copyright © 2002 by Andréa Wesson

The illustrations were executed in watercolor.
The text was set in 22-point Aunt Mildred.

For information about permission to reproduce selections
from this book, write to Permissions, Houghton Mifflin Company,
215 Park Avenue South, New York, NY 10003.
www.houghtonmifflinbooks.com
Printed in Malaysia

Library of Congress Cataloging-in-Publication Data
Weaver, Tess.
Opera cat / by Tess Weaver ; illustrated by Andréa Wesson.
p. cm.
Summary: When the opera diva Madame SoSo gets laryngitis,
her cat, Alma, fills in for her.
ISBN 0-618-09635-3
[1. Cats—Fiction. 2. Opera—Fiction. 3. Singers—Fiction. 4. Milan
(Italy)—Fiction. 5. Italy—Fiction.] I. Wesson, Andréa, ill. II. Title.
PZ7.G9483 Ni 2002
[E] 21   2001047574
TWP 10 9 8 7 6
4500236317

For Greg, with love
—T.W.

For Louise and the girls
—A.W.

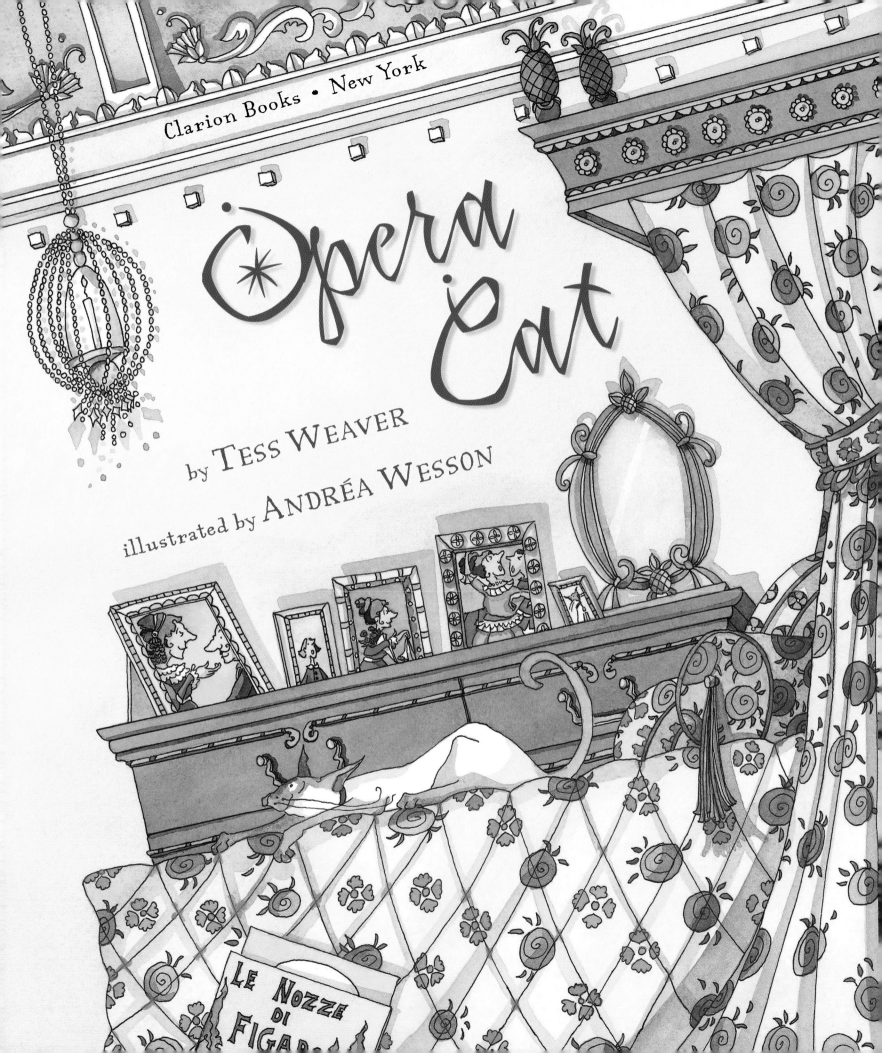

Clarion Books • New York

Opera Cat

by TESS WEAVER

illustrated by ANDRÉA WESSON

LE NOZZE DI FIGARO

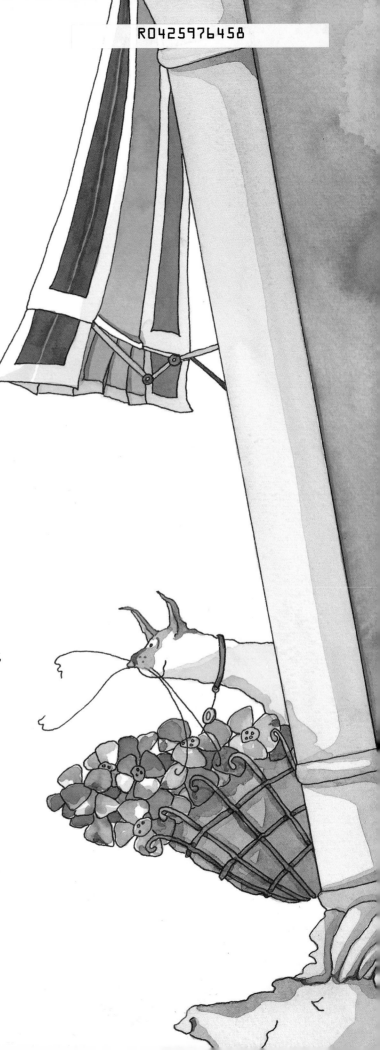

On Saturday morning, Alma sat on the windowsill of Madame SoSo's apartment licking her paws. It was an ordinary day. Alma looked out at Milan and noticed ordinary things.

Signora Gatti stood behind her street-cart, wrapping flowers in shiny paper. Shoppers strolled through the market, buying bread and cheese and fresh fish. A boy jumped into the fountain and was rescued by a woman wearing a red hat.

Alma wished she could jump down from her windowsill and explore the city. But her window was much too high. And Madame SoSo never took her out. Alma rubbed her cheek against the glass and sighed. Another ordinary day.

Or was it?

Here came Maestro walking toward the apartment to prepare Madame SoSo for her starring role in the opera. Maestro came every afternoon, but this time he was carrying roses!

Maestro worked Madame SoSo very hard. He made her sing deep, grumbling low notes, "Dum, dum, dum, deeee," and sharp, trembling high notes, "La, la, la, looo." Madame SoSo had to rest several times. She sat on the sofa, fanning herself with magazines while Maestro spritzed her throat with mineral water.

When they finished, Maestro kissed Madame SoSo's hand and called her "Cara." This was Alma's favorite part. She always peeked from behind the curtain to see the kiss.

If only Madame SoSo had looked behind the curtain even once during her practice, she would have realized that Alma was no ordinary cat.

For during every rehearsal with Maestro, Alma stood on her hind legs, clasping her paws and singing along in a soft whisper.

Alma loved the opera. Her amber eyes glowed as she lifted her furry chin and sang. She knew all the songs and practiced each time Maestro came. When he left, Maestro did not call Alma "Cara" or kiss her paw. But Alma always pretended that he did.

After dinner, Madame SoSo began to prepare for the night's performance. She took a long bath and curled her dark, thick hair. She put on shoes that made her look very tall and began to sing in front of the gold-leaf mirror.

"La, la, la, looo!" she tried. But this is what came out: "L - a l - u l - g l l." Her voice was cracking like an eggshell!

She cleared her throat and began again. This time only a whisper escaped her lips. "L-a-r-l-g l l."

Madame SoSo stared into the mirror and inspected her hot, red throat. Her reflection told her what she already knew. She had laryngitis!

12

Madame SoSo tore at her hair and paced the room. She drank a cup of hot water and a cup of cold water. She gargled salt water and stamped her feet. When she cried, enormous tears the size of coins dropped from her eyes.

But no matter how hard she tried, Madame SoSo could not sing a single note.

Alma, being a kind-hearted cat, could not bear to see Madame SoSo in such agony. She leapt onto the marble-top table, stood on her hind legs, and began singing.

"Caro nome che il mio cor!"

This was the first time Alma had ever dared to sing out loud. Her velvety voice filled the room with music.

Madame SoSo lifted her head, blinking her eyes as if waking from a dream.

Alma continued. *"Festi primo palpitar."*

What a voice! It was the voice of an angel, the voice of a devil. The voice of the stars and the moon, the oceans and the forests. Madame SoSo had never heard anything so lovely, so beautiful . . . *so much like her own!*

That night, for the first time since she was a kitten, Alma left the apartment. She hurried down the steps beside Madame SoSo, scratched her claws against a tree, and climbed into a limousine.

On the way to the opera, Alma stuck her pink nose out the window and smelled wonderful aromas: daisies and roses, mud and motorcycles, pizza cooking in brick ovens, water spraying from fountains, and all sorts of cats and dogs and people.

She watched the wheels on the limousine glide over the road. What a thrill to move without walking, to feel the cool misty air blow against her fur and hear the sound of wild wind in her ears.

Madame SoSo, meanwhile, was wondering how to hide Alma. How could Alma sing in the opera without anyone discovering their secret?

In her dressing room, Madame
SoSo tried hiding Alma under her
dress, behind her back, tucked in a
pocket. Finally, she put Alma on top
of her head. She practiced walking.
Alma practiced holding on without
using her claws.

Madame SoSo piled her hair into an immense tower of curls. Soon Alma was hidden and their secret was safe.

Just before the show, Maestro came to wish Madame
SoSo luck. When he kissed her cheek, he thought he
heard her purring. "Cara," he said, and kissed her again.

23

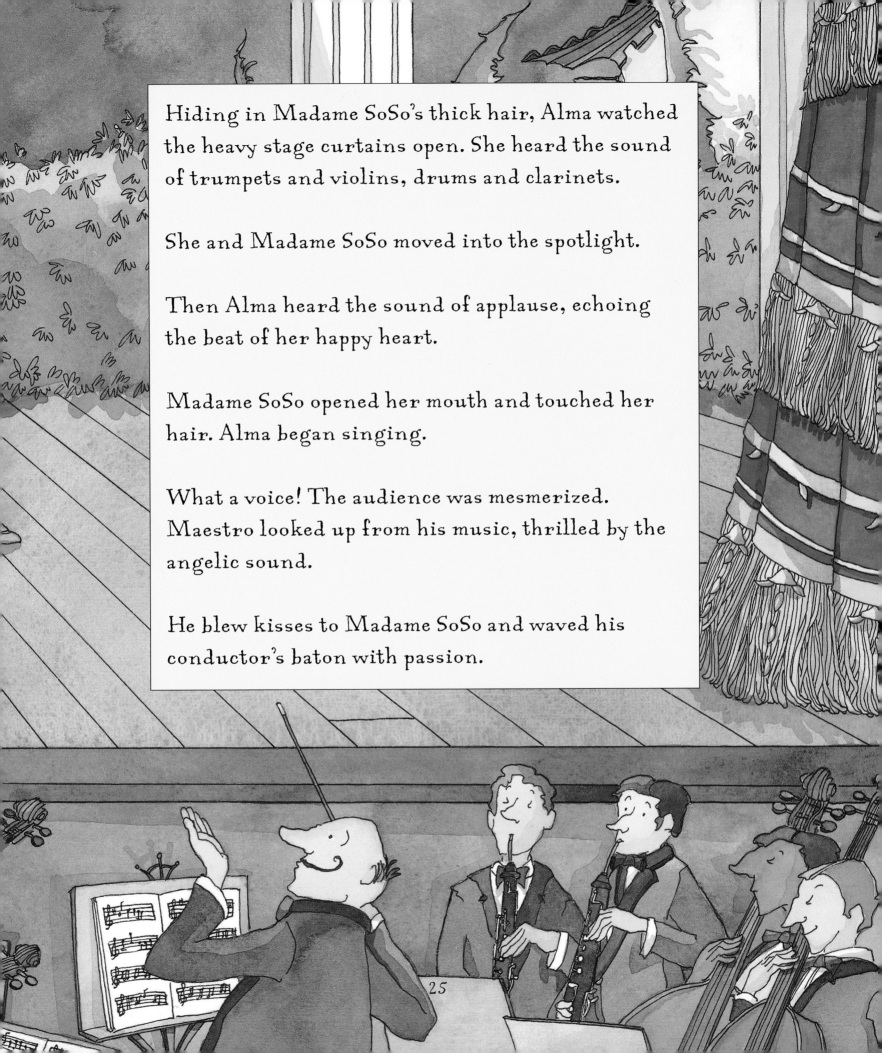

Hiding in Madame SoSo's thick hair, Alma watched the heavy stage curtains open. She heard the sound of trumpets and violins, drums and clarinets.

She and Madame SoSo moved into the spotlight.

Then Alma heard the sound of applause, echoing the beat of her happy heart.

Madame SoSo opened her mouth and touched her hair. Alma began singing.

What a voice! The audience was mesmerized. Maestro looked up from his music, thrilled by the angelic sound.

He blew kisses to Madame SoSo and waved his conductor's baton with passion.

But it was Alma who was singing, Alma who was applauded, Alma who was the star! Madame SoSo and Alma had tricked them all.

The audience cheered, "Brava! Bravissima!" Flowers
from the balcony, from the box seats, from center stage
rained down on the opera star.

As Madame SoSo bowed before the crowd, her magnificent tower of hair began to tremble and shake. Alma slipped forward, then back, and finally tumbled out in a long lock of hair, landing just behind Madame SoSo's right shoe.

No one saw the little cat. But Madame SoSo felt
her there, hiding behind her dress.

She lifted Alma out into the spotlight and kissed
her. The audience was amazed to see Madame SoSo
take her final bows with a cat in her arms.

29

After that night, Madame SoSo and
Alma were seen all over town—

strolling through the market, taking in the sights, sunbathing
in the park, dining al fresco, buying beautiful flowers.

And though Madame SoSo soon
recovered from her sore throat
and sang divinely, Alma attended
every opera . . .

just in case!

32